BOYSIE'S KITTEN

by Gillian Osband

pictures by Jonathan Allen

Carolrhoda Books, Inc./Minneapolis

This edition first published 1990 by Carolrhoda Books, Inc.
Originally published by Macmillan Children's Books, London.

LIBRARY OF CONGRESS CATALOGING-IN-PUBLICATION DATA

Osband, Gillian.
Boysie's kitten/by Gillian Osband.
p. cm.
Summary: Shunned by the three big ginger cats, Boysie the dog makes friends with K-fer the kitten.
ISBN 0-87614-403-2 (lib. bdg.) :
[1. Dogs—Fiction. 2. Cats—Fiction. 3. Friendship—Fiction.]
I. Title.
PZ7.0787Bp 1990
[E]—dc20 89-22168
CIP
AC

Manufactured in the United States of America

1 2 3 4 5 6 7 8 9 10 99 98 97 96 95 94 93 92 91 90

Boysie is a terrier.
She has to live with
three huge ginger cats.

To Boysie, the three huge ginger cats seem like lions.

They snarl,

show their nasty pointed teeth,

swish their tails in the air,
and they box!

But worst of all, the three huge ginger cats chase Boysie around her house and around her yard. Poor Boysie!

One day Boysie had been chased into the yard by one of the three huge ginger cats. As soon as she ran outside, she heard a squeak. It came from behind one of the flower pots.

Her ears perked up, her nose twitched, and she barked twice.

She waited and listened.
She heard the squeak again.

She barked three times, then slowly crept around the flower pot.

Suddenly she found
herself face-to-face
with a tiny, tiny kitten.

The moment she saw the
kitten, Boysie loved him.

"I shall call him K-fer, K for Kitty," she barked to herself. "And he's my friend."

Then she picked him up,
carried him inside, and
put him in her basket.

The three huge ginger cats ignored them.

Boysie showed K-fer
how to play
all sorts of games.
They played boxing,
leaping on plants,
and bump-the-slipper.

They played and played.
Boysie jumped on K-fer,

and K-fer jumped on Boysie.

They played nose-ball
with a roll of toilet paper,
and bury-the-pencil.

Boysie showed K-fer how to chew up newspapers and how to beg for food.

Boysie shared her toys
with K-fer.

She even showed him
where her bones were hidden
around the house.

The three huge ginger cats still ignored K-fer, so Boysie taught him how to play tricks on them. They played surprise pounce, catch-the-tail, and steal-the-food.

But one day
K-fer did a super-somersault
pounce onto . . .
Boysie!

And he did a spectacular
catch-the-tail on . . .
Boysie!

Boysie was angry with K-fer
and wouldn't play with him
anymore.

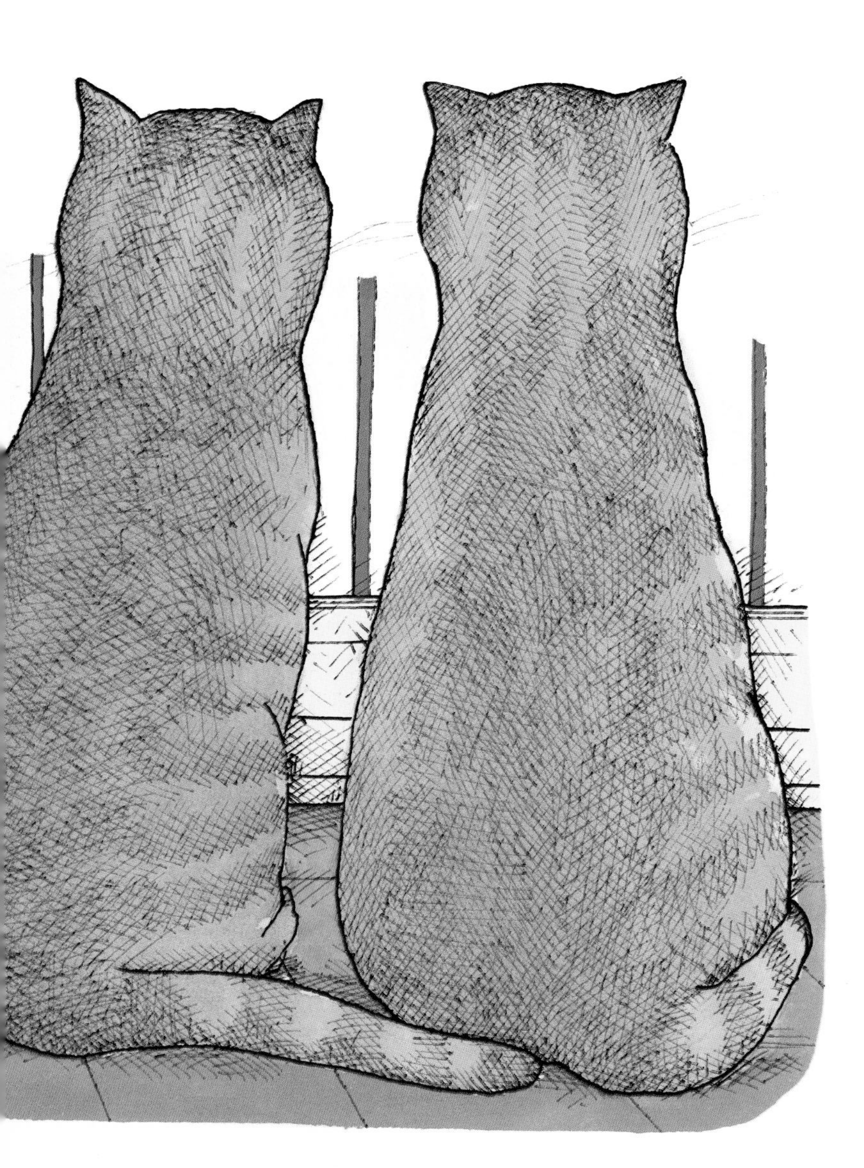

And the three huge ginger cats turned their backs on both of them.

K-fer went off on his own and cried.

K-fer knew he had been naughty, and now he felt sorry. He brought Boysie her biggest bone. But Boysie didn't want it.

Then K-fer had an idea.
It was suppertime for the cats.

K-fer sneaked around
the door and saw
Boysie's favorite food!
He decided to steal
some for her.

One of the three huge ginger cats saw Boysie
licking the food from her lips
and whacked her on the nose!

Boysie ran to her basket, and
K-fer followed her.
Boysie scrunched up a
special place for him.

"After all," barked Boysie to herself,
"K-fer is my friend."